To ....

For being good.

MERRY CHRISTMAS!

From Santa

"Ho, ho, ho!"
laughed Santa.

"Merry Christmas, Cleveland!"

Santa divided the carrots among all the reindeer.
"Well done!" he said, patting the youngest reindeer gently on the nose.

But the youngest reindeer didn't hear him...he was too busy munching!

Then it was time to set off for home. Santa reset his Santa-nav once more to the
North Pole, and soon they were speeding high above Riverside, past the Rock and Roll
Hall of Fame, and out over Rockefeller Park through the crisp, starry night.

Finally, Santa had delivered the last present on his long Cleveland list.

"Great moons and stars!" sighed Santa. "It's past midnight and my sack seems as heavy as ever! I hope I haven't forgotten anyone."

Santa opened his sack to check...but it was full of juicy, crunchy carrots!

Santa delivered presents to Abigail, Addison, Aiden, Alexander, Andrew, Ava... the list went on and on! ...Violet, Wyatt, Xavier, Zachary, Zoe, Zybil.

(Zybil? That must be a spelling mistake, surely!)

From Shaker Square to Detroit Shoreway, from Old Brooklyn to Ohio City, from Mount Pleasant to Forest Hill, from South Broadway to North Collinwood, and ALL the places in between, Santa and his sleigh visited every house in Cleveland.

Santa took a little bite out of each cookie, a tiny sip of milk, wiped his beard, and popped the carrots into his sack.

In house after house, the good children of Cleveland had left out a plate of cookies, a small glass of milk, and a big, crunchy carrot.

He piled them under the Christmas trees and carefully filled up the stockings with surprises.

In house after house, Santa delved inside his sack for packages of every shape and size.

The youngest reindeer was amazed at how quickly they went. Santa never seemed to get tired at all! And it looked like all the children in Cleveland were going to be very lucky this year! But the youngest reindeer was starting to feel a bit weary and quite hungry too!

Santa drove his sleigh expertly from rooftop to rooftop all over Cleveland, popping in and out of chimneys as fast as he could go.

(Which was pretty fast for a chubby fellow!)

There were big chimneys in Tremont and small chimneys in Lee-Miles. He squeezed down thin chimneys in West Park and plummeted down fat chimneys in Central.

Luckily, there
was no real
damage done, but
the packages had all
been jumbled up. Santa
quickly sorted out the
presents into order again.

"All right," said Santa. "Thanks
to this young reindeer I know where
we are now. Don't worry, children,

Santa is coming!"

The reindeer *pulled* with all their might until, at last, with a screeching noise, the sleigh scraped clear of the Christmas tree. Santa steered them safely above FirstEnergy Stadium, over the Cuyahoga River, above the West Side Market, and down into Lakewood Park.

Finally, when the snow had died down
and the clouds parted, Santa discovered
exactly where they were...

...stuck, right at the very top of a
Christmas tree in
Public Square!

"Everybody,
PULL!"

The sleigh hit something as it plummeted through the snow clouds. **"You have arrived!"** said the Santa-nav unhelpfully.

"Whoa!"

cried Santa, pulling his hat straight. "What's going on?" Then, to his surprise, he heard the ringing sound.

"Well done, young reindeer!" he shouted cheerfully, "It must be the bells of Trinity Cathedral. Don't worry, children, Santa is coming!"

Then, suddenly...

CRUNCH!

Ding-dong! Ding-dong!

There was that sound again, like church bells ringing. The youngest reindeer turned around to look at Santa. But Santa wasn't listening. He seemed to be arguing with a little box with buttons on it.

With a flick of the harness and a jerk of the reins, the youngest reindeer gave a sharp *tug* and headed off toward the sound of the bells, pulling Santa and his sleigh behind him!

Ding-dong!
Ding-dong!

Then, through the howling blizzard, the youngest reindeer heard a faint, ringing sound.

Ding-dong!

He looked over at the old reindeer with the red nose. But he had his head down.

(Red nose...I wonder who that could be?!)

Ding-dong!
Ding-dong!

They had just crossed Lake Erie
when, suddenly, they ran into a blizzard.
Snowflakes whirled around the sleigh.

They couldn't see a thing!

The youngest reindeer was getting a bit worried,
but Santa didn't seem concerned.

"In two miles..."

said the Santa-nav in a bossy lady's voice,

"...keep left at the next star."

"But, ma'am," Santa blustered, "I can't see any stars in all this snow!"
Soon they were

hopelessly lost!

Santa's sleigh flew through the starry night, heading south across the Arctic Ocean. On they flew in the crisp, wintry air, crossing over Canada. In the wink of an eye, the sleigh was flying above Michigan and on to Ohio. The youngest reindeer was very excited. He had never been away from the North Pole before.

"We'll soon have all these presents delivered to the Rock and Roll Capital of the World!"

With a flick of the reins and
a jerk of the harness, off they
went, racing through the sky.

"Ho, ho, ho!"
laughed Santa.

But the youngest reindeer was crunching so loudly that it was no wonder he hadn't heard the little old elf calling.

"Oh well, never mind," said Santa, giving the reindeer a little wink.
He took out his Santa-nav and tapped in the coordinates for Cleveland, Ohio.
"This will guide us to Cleveland in no time."

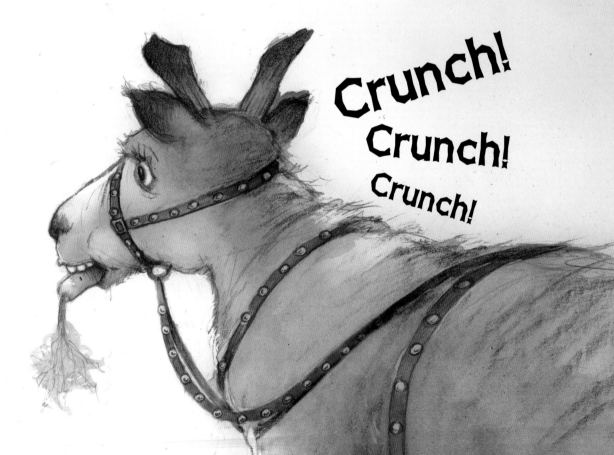

Crunch!
Crunch!
Crunch!

"Missing?

Which reindeer is missing?" asked Santa.

"The youngest one, Santa," said the elf. "It's his first flight tonight. I've called him and called him, but..."

Just then, a young reindeer strolled up, munching on a large carrot.

"Where have you been?"

asked Santa.

"Er...not quite, Santa," said the little old elf. "One of our reindeer is missing!"

Even though the sack of presents was

really, really big

and the elves were really, really small,

they seemed to have no trouble loading it onto Santa's sleigh.
Though how they managed to fit such a big sack into one little sleigh
even they didn't know. But somehow they did.

"Splendid!" boomed Santa. "We're ready to go!"

"Jolly good!" chuckled Santa,
"Then we'd better get their presents loaded up!"

"Well?"

boomed Santa. "Have all the children from **Cleveland** been good this year?"

"Well...uh...mostly," answered the little old elf, as he bustled across the busy workshop to Santa's desk.

Santa peered down at the elf from behind the tall, teetering piles of letters that the children of Cleveland had sent him.

"Mostly?" asked Santa, looking over the top of his glasses.

"Yes...but they've all been **especially** good in the last few days!" said the elf.

Santa is coming to Cleveland

Written by Steve Smallman
Illustrated by Robert Dunn

sourcebooks
jabberwocky

Written by Steve Smallman
Illustrated by Robert Dunn
Designed by Sarah Allen

Published by Sourcebooks Jabberwocky, an imprint of Sourcebooks, Inc.
P.O. Box 4410, Naperville, Illinois 60567-4410
(630) 961-3900
Fax: (630) 961-2168
www.jabberwockykids.com

Library of Congress Cataloging-in-Publication data is on file with the publisher.

Source of Production: Leo Paper Products, Guangdong Province, China
Date of Production: April 2014
Run Number: HTW_PO170314
Printed and bound in China
LEO 10 9 8 7 6 5 4 3 2 1

Santa is coming to Cleveland